A Grey Day in Toy Town

HarperCollins *Children's Books*

It was a grey day in Toy Town and a most peculiar cloud was approaching. Noddy was driving Tessie Bear and Bumpy Dog to the train station.

"We're taking the train out into the country to look at all the pretty wildflowers," Tessie explained to Noddy. "They come in so many different colours – and I just love colours!"

Tessie was so happy that she sang a song:

There's a world of colour
Made for you and me
Mixed up together
Oh so prettily

Pink and gold the sunset
Blue and green the sea
There's a world of colour
Made for you and me!

"I hope you haven't forgotten your umbrella, Tessie," said Noddy. "I saw the most peculiar cloud approaching Toy Town."

"I've got my umbrella right here – along with paper and crayons of all colours of the rainbow, so I can draw those wonderful flowers," replied Tessie Bear.

At the station, Noddy asked Tessie Bear which train was hers. "There are three trains here, a red one, a blue one and a green one. Which one is yours?"

"The blue one, of course – to match my bow!" Tessie Bear giggled.

"After you have seen all those pretty flowers, I hope Toy Town doesn't look dull and grey when you come back!" Noddy laughed. "Goodbye, Tessie Bear!"

"Goodbye, Noddy!" called Tessie Bear, and Bumpy Dog barked goodbye too.

As Noddy drove off he noticed the strange cloud again.

"Tessie Bear left just in time," he thought. "It looks like that cloud is about to burst! Let's go home, car."

In Toy Town, everyone else had noticed the weather too.

"There's that most peculiar cloud!" exclaimed Mr Jumbo, just as the rain started to pour.

"What is it doing?" wondered Clockwork Mouse.

The rain from the peculiar cloud was washing away all of the colours from Toy Town!

“Where did all the yellow on my car go?” gasped Noddy. “And my shirt – it’s not red anymore!”

Everyone was very worried and came out to talk about what was going on.

“The rain washed away all our colours! All we have left is black, white and grey!” cried Mr Jumbo.

Miss Pink Cat was very upset. "That rain has got into everything! My Red Googleberry Surprise ice cream is now Grey Googleberry Surprise – and that is not a very nice surprise!"

"You can say that again, Miss Pink Cat... or should I say, Miss Grey Cat?" said Mr Plod.

"Oh no!" Miss Pink Cat was not happy to find that she was no longer pink.

"This is a terrible day for Toy Town," agreed Mr Plod.

Meanwhile, Tessie Bear and Bumpy Dog were having a lovely day in the countryside, where it wasn't raining.

"What a wonderful day! So many pretty colours!" Tessie Bear said to Bumpy Dog.

"Look, Bumpy Dog, here's a drawing I did of those beautiful blue flowers we saw. And here are the red berries. Oh, and look at the green leaves!"

"Woof!" agreed Bumpy Dog.

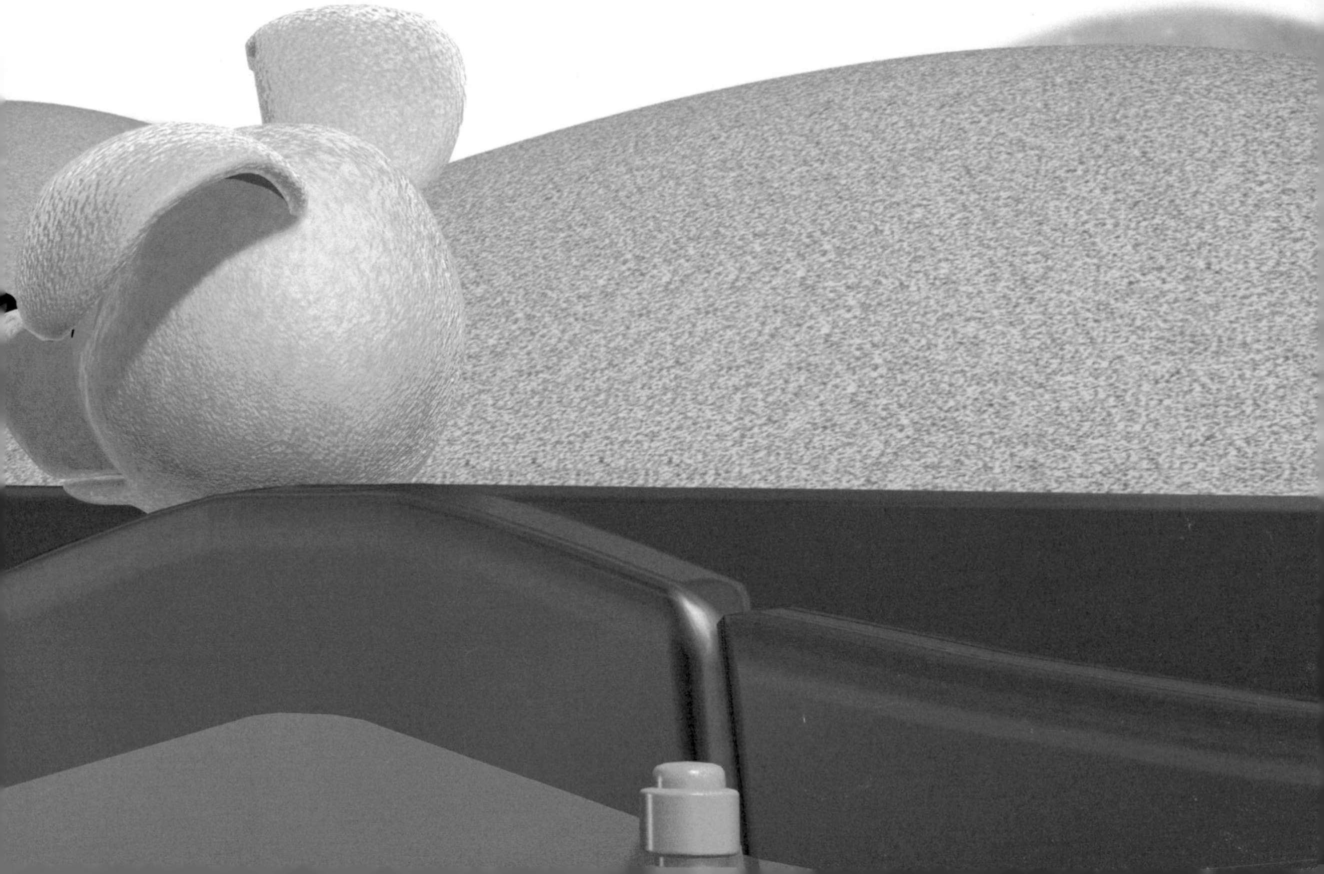

"Oh, Tessie Bear!" cried Noddy, when he saw Tessie Bear and Bumpy Dog back in Toy Town. "I'm sorry I forgot about your train. I was just on my way to pick you up!"

"I don't care about the taxi ride, Noddy! Where did all the lovely colours go?" Tessie asked.

"Remember that weird cloud this morning? Well, it rained on Toy Town and washed away all the colours!" Noddy explained, sadly.

"Except for you and Bumpy, that is."

"Noddy, we have to do something to bring back the colours!' cried Tessie Bear.

Noddy did not know what they could do, but Tessie Bear had an idea.

"Aha! I'm not grey, so maybe my crayons aren't grey either!"

Tessie Bear checked in her bag and saw that the crayons were still colourful.

Using Tessie's crayons, Noddy, Tessie Bear and Bumpy Dog started colouring in everything that had gone grey.

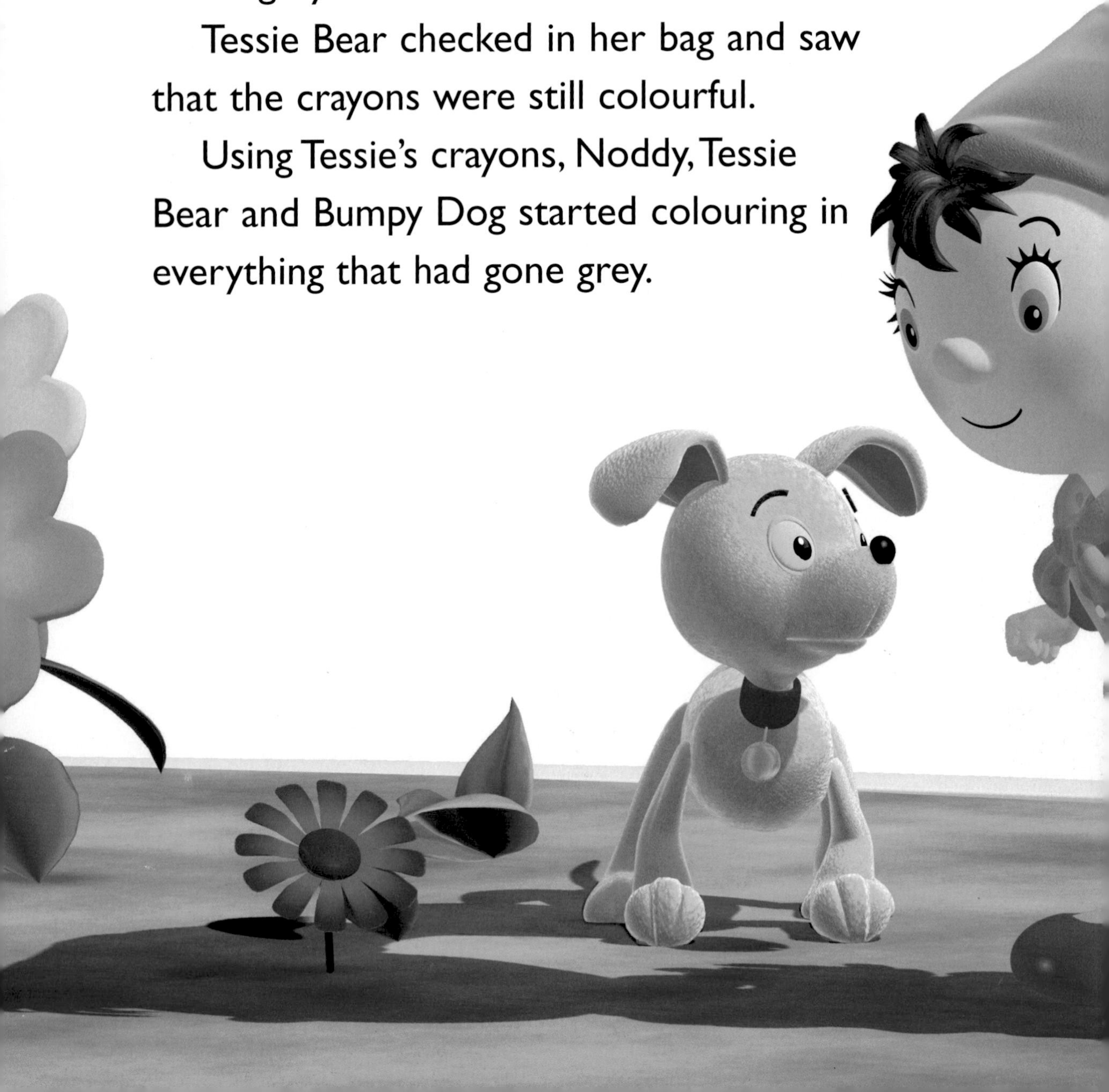

"Look, I'm making the flower blue!" said Noddy.

"And I'm making the lamppost green!" replied Tessie Bear.

But the friends soon realised that they didn't have enough crayons to colour the whole town.

"There's not even enough crayon to colour me!" Noddy said, sadly.

"We can't let Toy Town stay this way, Noddy," said Tessie Bear. "Oh, how I'd love to see some bright colours right now."

"Look, Tessie, over there!" Noddy said suddenly, pointing into the sky.

"Oooh, a rainbow!" said Tessie. "How – how – colourful! If only we could get that rainbow to share its colours with Toy Town!"

"Hmm..." thought Noddy. "We can! Let's grab a bucket and head for the airport!"

Tessie Bear did not know what Noddy's plan was, but she picked up a bucket and followed him and Bumpy Dog to the airport.

Soon, Noddy and his two friends spotted the rainbow from the plane. "Let's see if we can use some of its colour on my grey aeroplane," Noddy suggested. "Hold on!"

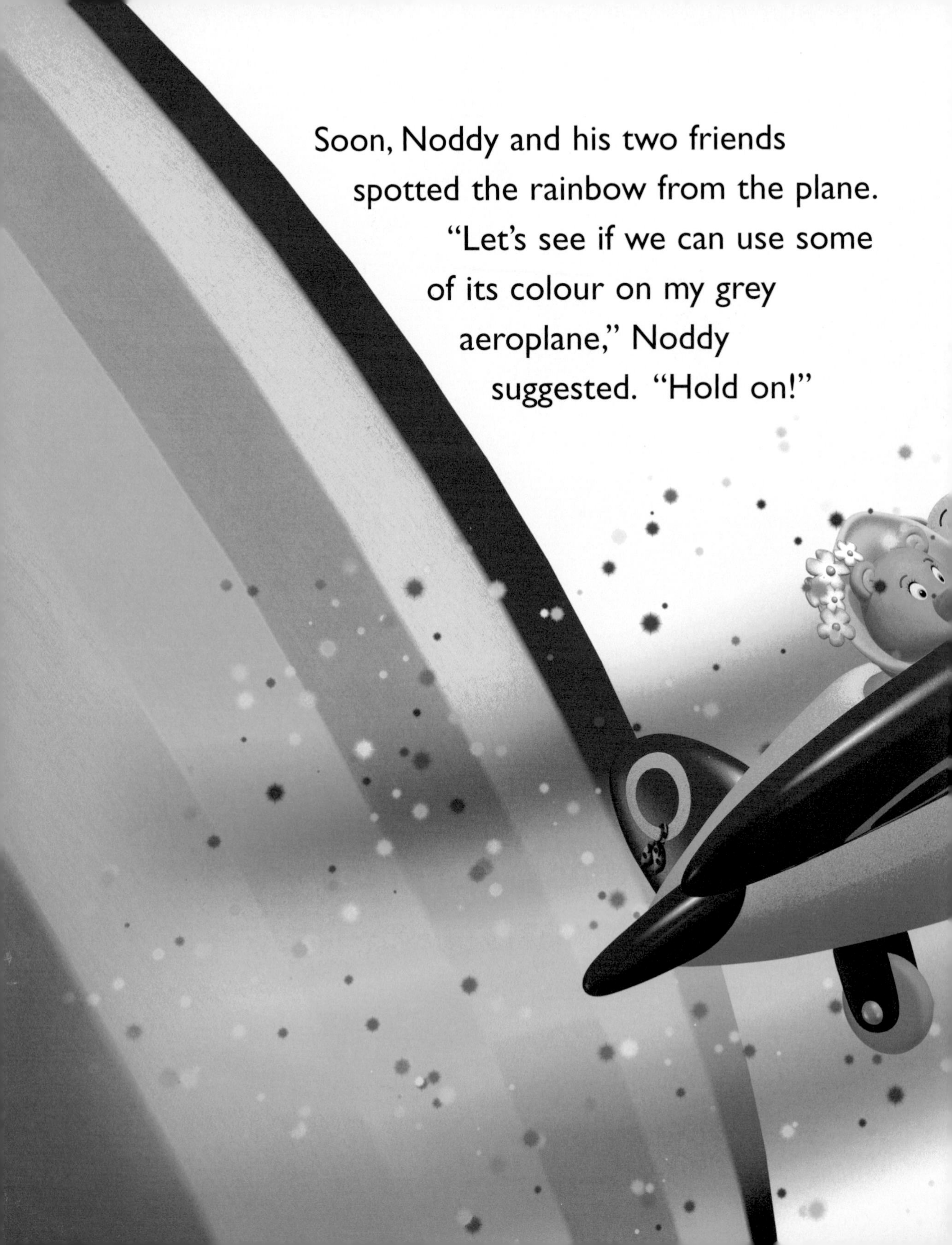

They swooped through the rainbow in the aeroplane.

"Your colours are back, Noddy! Hurray!" cheered Tessie Bear.

"Yes, my shirt is red again! It is, it is, it is!"

"I'm going to fly through the rainbow again," said Noddy. "This time, scoop up some of the colours with the bucket!" he instructed.

"I've got it, Noddy!" cried Tessie Bear, as she collected the colours in the bucket.

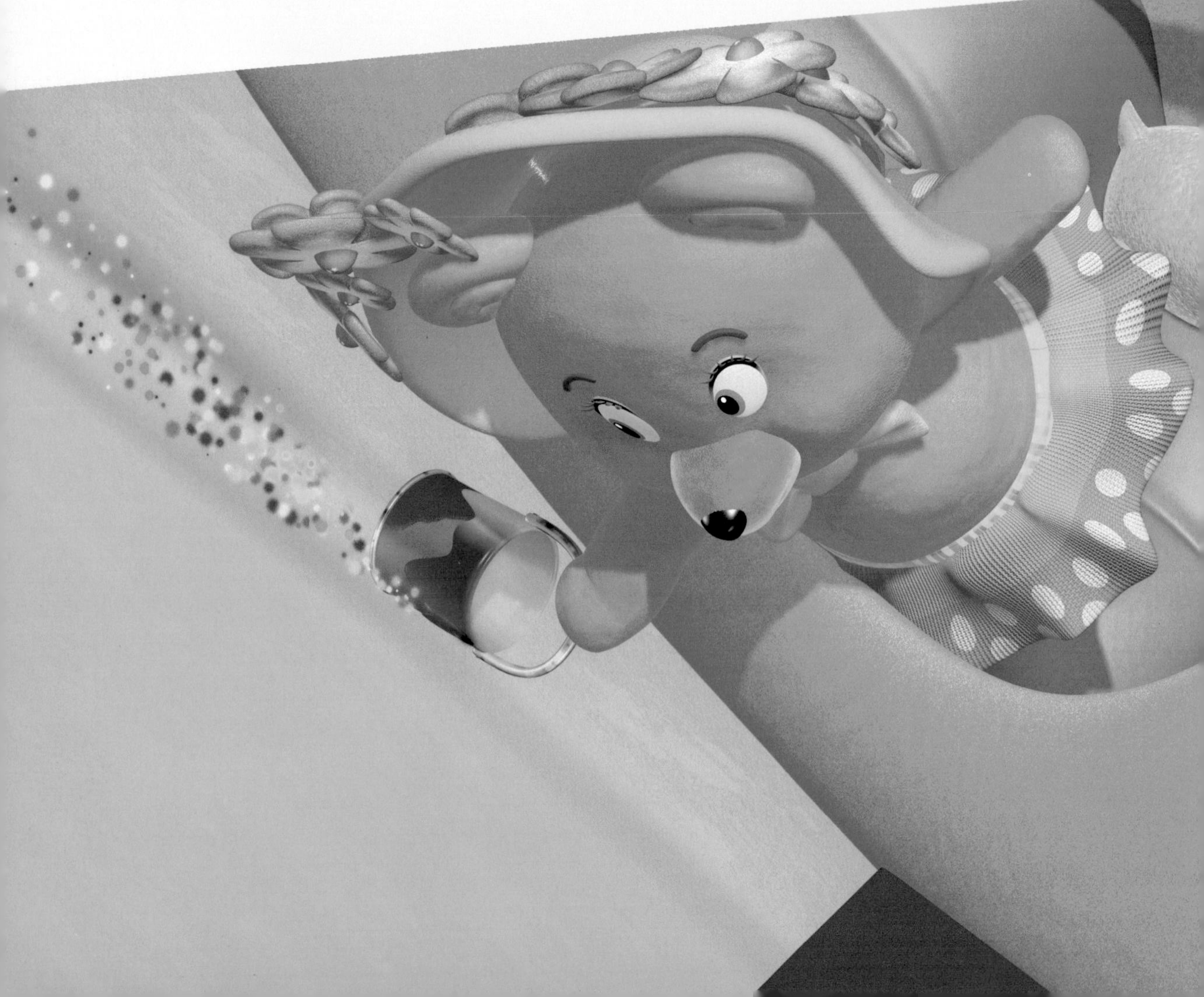

Noddy flew the aeroplane back towards Toy Town.

"All right, Tessie. There's Toy Town right under us. NOW, Tessie!" Noddy shouted.

Tessie emptied the bucket of rainbow colours all over Toy Town and everybody below had a wonderful surprise.

As the colours fell over Toy Town, they made everything look as beautiful as it had before. The sky became blue again, the trees green and everything grey was turned into a bright colour.

"Look," said Mr Wobbly Man. "We have our colours back!"

"And so have our shops!" Dinah Doll said, happily.

Everyone gave three cheers for Noddy and Tessie Bear.

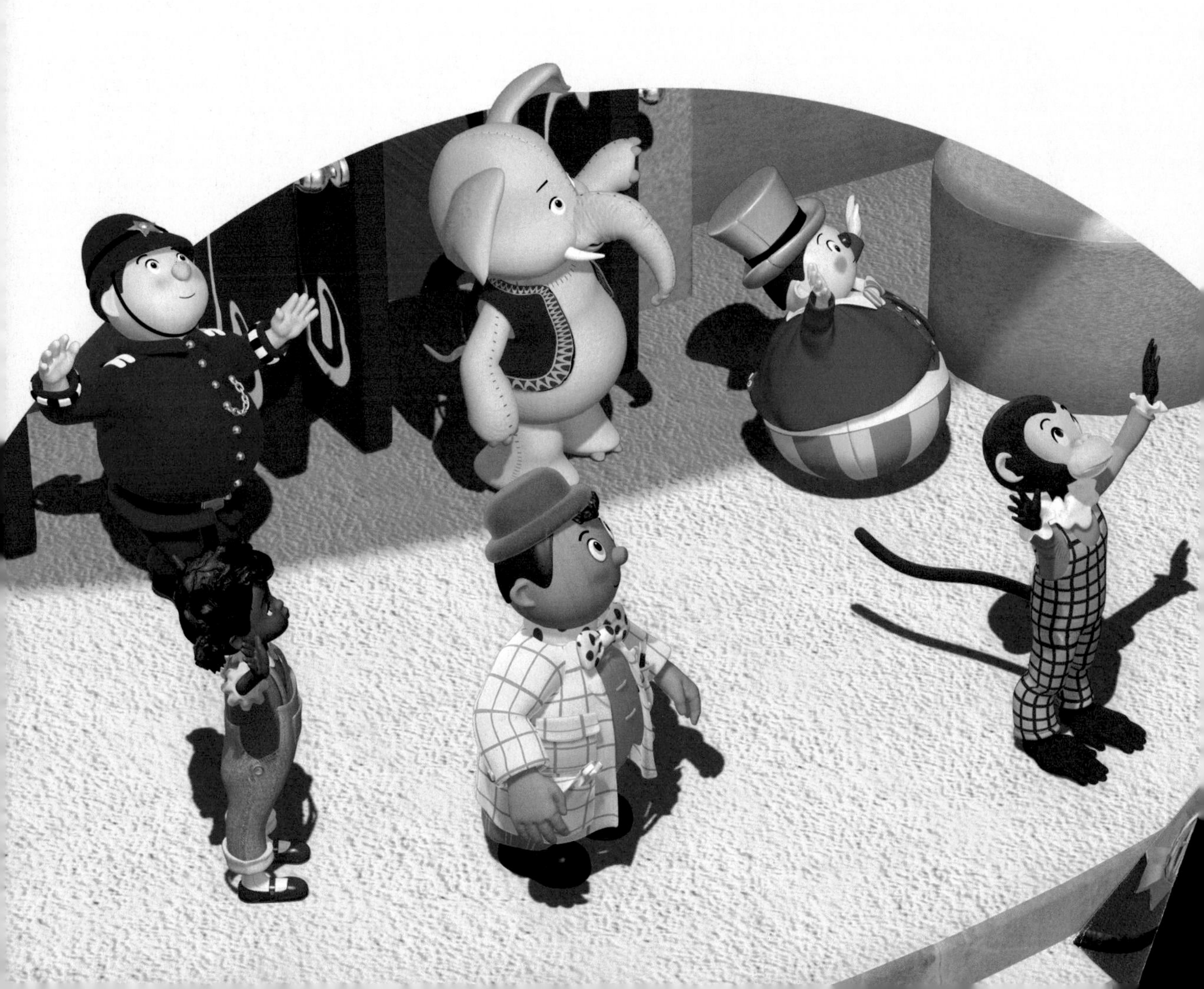

As Noddy flew to the airport to land the aeroplane, he saw Toy Town looking more beautiful than ever.

His House-for-One had a red roof again and the town hall steps were bright yellow as they used to be.

"Hurray!" cheered Noddy and Tessie Bear.

Later, on the town hall steps, Mr Plod thanked the three friends.

"On behalf of the entire town, I congratulate our heroes, Noddy and Tessie Bear."

"Woof!" barked Bumpy Dog.

"...and Bumpy Dog, too," laughed Mr Plod.

"I'm just glad that all the wonderful, beautiful colours have returned to Toy Town," said Tessie Bear.

"Yes," agreed Noddy. "Thank goodness we got rid of all that grey!"

"Hear, hear!" cheered Mr Plod.

Tessie looked around.

"Oh no!" she cried. "We forgot to colour Mr Jumbo! Get some crayons!"

"No, no, wait!" exclaimed Mr Jumbo. "I'm SUPPOSED to be grey!"

"Oh that's right. Sorry!" apologised Tessie Bear.

Everybody laughed, happy to be back to normal.

First published in Great Britain by HarperCollins Children's Books in 2006
HarperCollins Children's Books is a division of HarperCollins Publishers Ltd,
77-85 Fulham Palace Road, Hammersmith, London W6 8JB

1 3 5 7 9 10 8 6 4 2

For further information on Noddy and the Noddy Club please contact www.Noddy.com

ISBN 0-00-722336-6
ISBN-13 978-0-00-722336-7

A CIP catalogue for this title is available from the British Library.

The HarperCollins website address is:
www.harpercollinschildrensbooks.co.uk

Printed and bound by
Printing Express Ltd, Hong Kong